POPCORN BOB

IN AMERICA

IN AMERICA

MARANKE RINCK

illustrated by **MARTIJN VAN DER LINDEN**

translated by Nancy Forest-Flier

LEVINE QUERIDO

MONTCLAIR · AMSTERDAM · HOBOKEN

This is an Em Querido book
Published by Levine Querido

www.levinequerido.com · info@levinequerido.com

Levine Querido is distributed by Chronicle Books LLC

Originally published in the Netherlands by Querido

Library of Congress Control Number: 2022930812
ISBN 978-1-64614-174-6

Printed and bound in China

Published in August 2022
First Printing

Book design by Patrick Collins
The text type was set in Fresco Normal

Martijn van der Linden drew the illustrations for this book with a 2B pencil on 300 gsm paper while eating a mix of salty and sweet popcorn.

Popcorn Ella was inspired by a drawing by Annabelle van Tatenhove.

This publication has been made possible with financial support from the Dutch Foundation for Literature.

Nederlands letterenfonds
dutch foundation
for literature

POPCORN
BOB
IN AMERICA

Bill's
Popcorn
Farm

Farmer Bill sticks his nose in the air.
"Mmm..."
Summer smells better here than it does *anywhere* else.
Sweet corn.
Fresh manure.
Wonderful!
Bill takes another deep breath.

Maybe a little *too* deep.
Because now there's a fly up his nose.

"Get out of there, you," Bill mutters.
He blows his nose into a big handkerchief.

"Time to get to work."

"Grody, grisly goats!" he shouts a few minutes later.

"Back in the vacation house, I see.
Come on, out you go.
You, too. Scram!
I'm expecting guests."

Who'll need a place to sleep.

So you'll have to go camping for a while.

Come on now.
Don't make me mad.

MEEEH

Finally Bill can get started.
First he sweeps the floor till it shines.
Then he hangs a curtain in the window.
He gets rid of a spiderweb.
And turns a crate into a cute little table.
Working fast, he pumps some air into the air mattresses.
Pssst-pssst-pssst.
Now he's done.
Bill looks around the room and smiles.
"Super-deluxe," he says.
"It's like a five-star hotel in here."

Meh?
PFFF!
PFFF!
meeeh!
Bill's
popcorn
farm
meeeh!

AIRPORT

CHAPTER 1

I KNOW PERFECTLY WELL WHO BOB IS

This is my honest face.
Not bad, huh?

You see that sweet smile?
Those happy eyes?
I've worked on it for a long time.
This is the face of an ordinary nine-year-old girl.
NOT the face of a phony.

Dante is trying to look well-behaved, too.
That's not hard.
He's sleeping like a baby.

Okay.
He sounds more like a baby *pig*.
But that's okay, because we're in America!

POPCORN LAND!

We've succeeded with Step One of our plan.

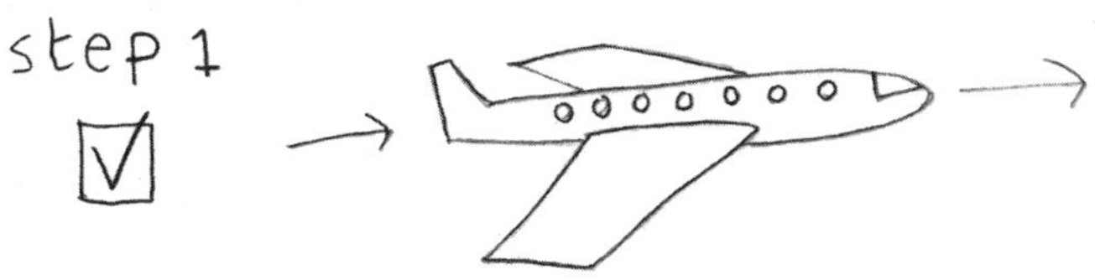

Now it's time for Step Two.

We're going to stay with Farmer Bill.

And my fathers are going to work for him.

Then comes Step Three.

Dante and I are going ON VACATION!
At least…
That's what my fathers think.
But of course that's not true.
Dante and I have no time for vacation.
No, Step Three is a secret.
A huge secret.
Only Farmer Bill knows what it is.
And nobody else.

My fathers don't know anything about it.
Which is just as well.
They have enough on their minds.
Such as: what's keeping Bill?
He's supposed to pick us up from the airport.
But we've been waiting an hour already.

They've gone around the corner to have a quick look.
Now I can take a peek in my bag.

Bob has been hiding in there for hours.
The WHOLE way, from Holland to America.

Without whining!
And he hasn't gotten mad, not even once.
I really didn't think he had it in him.
I'm SO proud.
It makes me feel all warm inside.
"Hey," I whisper.
I bend way over.
"Hey, Bob.
Buddy...
We're almost there!
Just a few more..."

Oh, no!
My backpack is wide open.
Like a big, gaping mouth.

And it's empty.

POPCORN BOB! I roar, but only in my head.
You broke your promise!
I straighten myself up.
That nice, warm, proud feeling is gone in a flash.
The sun is shining bright.
But I'm freezing cold.
"*ZZZZZZ!*" Dante snores again.
"Hey, cut it OUT, DANTE!" I snarl.
I give him a poke.
Dante opens his eyes.
"Huh?" he mutters.

"Bob," I tell him.
Dante gives me a goofy look.
"Bob?"

I completely forget to whisper.

Dante gives his head a rub.
"Take it easy," he mumbles.

"Well," I say.
"He's gone."

CHAPTER 2

NOT A MARACA

"Bob is gone?"
Dante sits straight up.
I nod.
I gaze across the parking lot.
At the cars and the sidewalk.
At the row of chairs...

"Where could he be?" I mutter.
Suddenly I see something moving.
I groan.

“You’ve GOT to be kidding me!”

Dante follows my gaze.
Bob isn't far away.
He's in the vending machine.
He's *INSIDE of it!*
Along with the bags of chips and cookies.
He looks very happy.

Dante and I grab our bags.
We run to the machine.
But we aren't alone.

A little girl has beat us to it.
She starts pushing the buttons really fast.
As if she does this every day.
I gasp.
My fathers NEVER let me eat food from vending machines.
Not even if it's popcorn.
Whoop, a cookie drops down.
Plunk-click!
The girl takes it out of the tray.

She holds the cookie up and shouts something.
In English.
"What did she say?" I ask Dante.
"She said somebody has taken a bite out of her cookie," he translates.

The little girl runs away.
And Bob is still there, behind the glass.
He's chewing and swallowing.
Pretending he can't see me.
I tap on the vending machine window.
I'm really mad.
"Somebody will see you."

Get out of there,
RIGHT NOW.

Suddenly the little girl is standing next to us.
She sticks *another* coin into the vending machine.
The machine pushes Bob forward.
And then drops him down.
As if he were a cookie too.
Bonk!

The girl snatches Bob from the tray.
She pokes him in the tummy.
And she mutters something.
"She wants to know where the candy is," Dante whispers.
"Candy?
What candy?" I ask.
Dante shrugs.

Bob looks angry.
And then even angrier.
And then…

"HEY, CHICKEN HEAD!" he roars suddenly.

I'm a corn kernel
Not a maraca!

The girl stares at Bob.
Before she can say anything, I snatch him out of her hands.
She glares at me.
"Grrrr," she says.
And even though I can't speak English,
I know exactly what she says next:
"That's mine!"
"No, it's not," I say in Dutch.
I whisper to Dante:

You've got money, haven't you? Get her something out of that vending machine.

Dante has a bunch
of coins.
He got them from his
American mother.

He gets the girl a new cookie.
But she shakes her head no.
She points to my hands.
I hold them up.
“I haven’t got anything,” I tell her.
Bob is now safely hidden under my shirt.

Dante groans.
“Now she says we’ve stolen her dolly.
Uh-oh, here comes her mother.”

CHAPTER 3

I DON'T HAVE ANYTHING, HONEST!

I cover Bob with my hands, hoping he
won't be noticed.
But the woman isn't even looking at me.
She's examining the vending machine.
Row by row.
Chips, bags of candy,
chocolate bars, cookies…
She shakes her head.
"She says there are no dolls
in there," Dante whispers.
The girl turns
bright red.
She points
to me.

I take a step back.
"Uh…Dante," I say.
"Should we go?"
Suddenly Bob pokes me in the stomach.
It almost knocks me over.
"Ellis," he moans.
"HUNGRY!"
His poke really tickles!
I try to stifle my laughter, but it's impossible.

Now the mother IS looking at me.
She narrows their eyes.
"I don't have anything, honest!" I yell.

I show them first one empty hand.
And then the other.

I smile sweetly.
And I flutter my eyelashes.
The mother nods.
I turn around.
Phew.
What would I do without my honest face?

Dante and I race back to our chairs.
But Bob hasn't given up.
He keeps squirming under my hands.
"Just COOPERATE a little longer," I hiss.
I squeeze him even tighter.
But he's starting to tremble.
And buzz.

He's getting hotter and hotter.
Bigger and bigger.
And then…

Bob comes shooting out of my shirt.
As if I were a pan without a lid.
He's turned into an enormous piece of white popcorn.
"Ellis, here comes your father," Dante says quickly.
And he's right. On top of *everything* else!

Bob dives under a chair.
You'd think he'd keep his mouth shut for once.
But no.
He wails like a spoiled kid.
Dante and I stand in front of him.
"Hi, Dad," I say loudly.
"Hey, Gus," says Dante.
"We're coming!"

Luckily the little girl at the vending machine is bawling, too.
"WAAAAH!" she screams.
Her face is purple!
My father looks at her in amazement.
He's not paying attention to us anymore.
And he can't hear Bob either.
"Well, that's what happens," he mutters.

Candy makes kids hyper.

I drop to my knees and grab Bob with both hands. Bolts of lightning are shooting out of his eyes.

I shove him into my bag without saying a word.
"Haven't forgotten anything?" my father asks.
"Bill and Steve are around the corner."
"No, I've got everything," I say.

Hi, Ellis.

CHAPTER 4

YES MEANS JA

My fathers are sitting up front, next to Bill.
Dante and I are in the back with the suitcases and bags.
Bill shouts something to us.
"*Hold on tight!*" Steve translates.
I wrap my arms around my backpack.
The engine roars like a monster.
Dante laughs.
"Woo-hoo, here we go!" he says.
The truck tears around a bend.
And we go rolling against our luggage.

All this bouncing.
I HATE bouncing!

Bill turns onto the highway.
Dante and I shove some of the bags together.
Now we've got a kind of wall.
I look at the rearview mirrors and nod.
"I don't think they can see us now."
Bob sticks his head out of my bag.
"Have you calmed down?" I ask.
"Yes," says Bob, in English.
"And I can speak pretty good English, too.
Almost as good as my Dutch.
Did you hear that?"

“Just a little further and we’re there,” I say.
“I don’t think the farm is very far away.”
I peer over the side of the pickup.
Endless fields of corn are gliding by.
Little yellow tufts are pointing straight up like fingers.
Bob is balancing on the edge of the truck.
Suddenly he holds his arms out wide.

"Come here," I say.
I stick out my hand and Bob steps onto my palm.
"We've come here for *you*. You remember that, right?" I say.
Bob looks at the pile of junk we're sitting on.
"Not HERE, in the truck," I say.
"I mean: here, in AMERICA."
Bob nods.
"And why did you want to come here so badly?" I go on.

Bob gives me a look of shock.
"Have you forgotten already?

Fine, then I'll remind you AGAIN."

You made me in the microwave. Thanks, by the way.
Then you told the popcorn factory about me. Not a smart move.
And then the boss of the factory wanted to kidnap me.
Of course that didn't work.
But she said she had MORE living corn kernels.
Here, in America.
Dante overheard that.
Right, Dante?

"So we're on the same page," I say. "I'm here to help YOU!"

"Yes," says Bob (in English, of course).
He winks.
"You're a really nice girl.
Not like that kid at the airport.
Who kept pointing at you with her weird little fingers!"
I roll my eyes.
"But why did you run away?"
Bob gives me a big grin.
"I saw pink cookies."

"You love ALL cookies!" I shout.
"Pink, green, yellow..."

"Well, that's true," says Bob.
"Do you have one for me?"
I try not to laugh.
"Ellis," Dante says suddenly.

"Oh, no, there she is!" Bob shouts.
"Coraline Corn," I say.
"Unbelievable.
We were just talking about her!"
The big semi-truck behind us speeds up.
Coraline's enormous head shoots past.
Farmer Bill honks his horn.

"Whoa. She really is the creepiest woman I know," I sigh.

"Very creepy," says Dante.

"I DO NOT LIKE HER!" shouts Bob.

We turn off the highway onto a side road.

First we drive down a muddy track.

Then Bill pulls into a farmyard.

We're there!

Bob jumps into my bag.

CHAPTER 5

WOW, TAKE A LOOK AT THAT!

Bill's farmhouse is small.
But the yard around it is big.
And the cornfields around the yard are gigantic.
Gus clears his throat.
"Wow, take a look at that!" he says.
"Yes," says Steve.
"So, uh... this is it?"

"It's great," I say quickly.
I smile at Bill.
"Shall we go in?"
My fathers don't even hear me.
"I guess this is typical America," Steve whispers.

With all this stuff lying around.
It's really kind of cozy.

"I think it's wonderful," I say.
I drag my suitcase to the front door.
Bill grins and holds me back.
He points to a little wooden building.

“Oh, I get it,” Steve says.
“Ellis and Dante sleep in the guest house.
Dad and I sleep in the main farmhouse.”
He looks anxiously at the shack.

It looks more like a tree house than a guest house.
A really *old* tree house.
Without the tree.
Gus sighs.
“No, you two can sleep in our room in the farmhouse.
And we’ll sleep in that, uh... hut.”
“No way,” I say.
“We’ll take the hut.
Come on, Dante.”

Bill comes along with us.
He opens the door.
Three goats come running out.
Dante and I jump aside.
Bill hurls a few angry words at the goats.
Then he looks at us with a laugh.
"Bobby?" he asks.
I nod and walk into the hut.
"Here he is."
I unzip my bag.

Bill is crazy about Bob.
And Bob loves Bill.
They haven't seen each other in a very long time.
Not since Bill was in Holland.
So Dante and I leave them alone.

The air mattresses are flat, so we pump them up.
Then I open the shutters a crack.
That makes it nice and cozy.
Bill has even put a tablecloth over a crate.
"Hey, Dante," I say.
"Ask Bill when he's taking us to the popcorn factory."

Dante discusses this with Bill.
Boy, do I wish I could speak English!
I can't understand a thing they say.
But Bob?
He's nodding his head enthusiastically!
"You can't really understand him, can you?" I ask.
"Shhh," Bob whispers.
"Not if you keep talking!"

Didn't I tell you I speak really good Englisch?

"Bill is taking us to the factory tomorrow," Dante translates.

"He says he's going to chat with your fathers now.
To show them where everything is.
Later he'll bring food for Bob."
Bob nods.

Fantastic.
I understood every word.

"You're so smart," I say.
But I don't believe him for a second.
Bill goes outside.
"Make sure there's plenty to eat!" Bob calls after him (in Dutch, of course).

CHAPTER 6

WAY COOL

My fathers are deep in conversation.
They look like corn kernels that are *almost* ready to explode.
"What's the matter?" I ask.
"Ellis," Gus begins.
Drops of sweat roll off his forehead.
"All of this…"
He makes a circle with his hand.

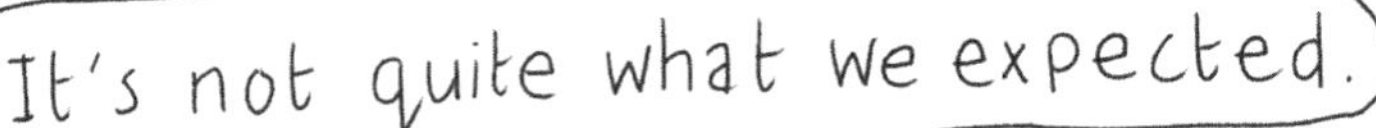

I raise my eyebrows.
"Is it too warm?"
"No," says Gus.
"Well... it *is* warm.
But I mean Bill's farm."
"I have no idea what you mean," I say.
Steve smiles.
"Let me put it this way:
If this farm was a boat, it would sink."

Gus grins.
"If it was an umbrella,
and it rained, you'd
get soaked!"

My fathers both laugh.
"I sure wouldn't mind a little rain right now," says Gus, gasping for air.
"What are you TALKING about?" I ask.
"It's just a nice old farm."
Gus wipes his forehead with his hand.
"Whew," he puffs.
"That feels better."
He takes a deep breath.
"But seriously.
We didn't know Bill was struggling like this."
I shrug my shoulders.
"So?"

"It's not fair," says Steve.
An angry look comes over his face.
"Bill has worked with the popcorn factory for years.
And this is all he's got to show for it!"
Gus nods.
"We really want to help him.
But we don't want to trouble him.
He just doesn't have room for us.
We're sleeping in a closet, Ellis.
And your hut is..."
"PERFECT," I say.
I kiss the tips of my fingers.
"We'll come take a look," says Steve.
Then I remember Bob.

I quickly shake my head.
"Oh, you don't have to do that.
It's really a cool little house!"
I turn to Dante.

I feel like an idiot.
I know perfectly well that it's a goat shed.
Gus is already standing up.
"Now I'm really curious!"
I put on my honest face.
"Listen," I say calmly.
"This is OUR HUT.
No fathers allowed."
"I was the same with my parents," says
Steve with a grin.
"Kids love secrets."
I laugh along with him.
He has no idea.

Dante gives me a nudge.
"There's Bill," he says.
"Go talk to him," I whisper to Dante.
"My fathers will want to go to a hotel or something.
We can't do that with Bob."

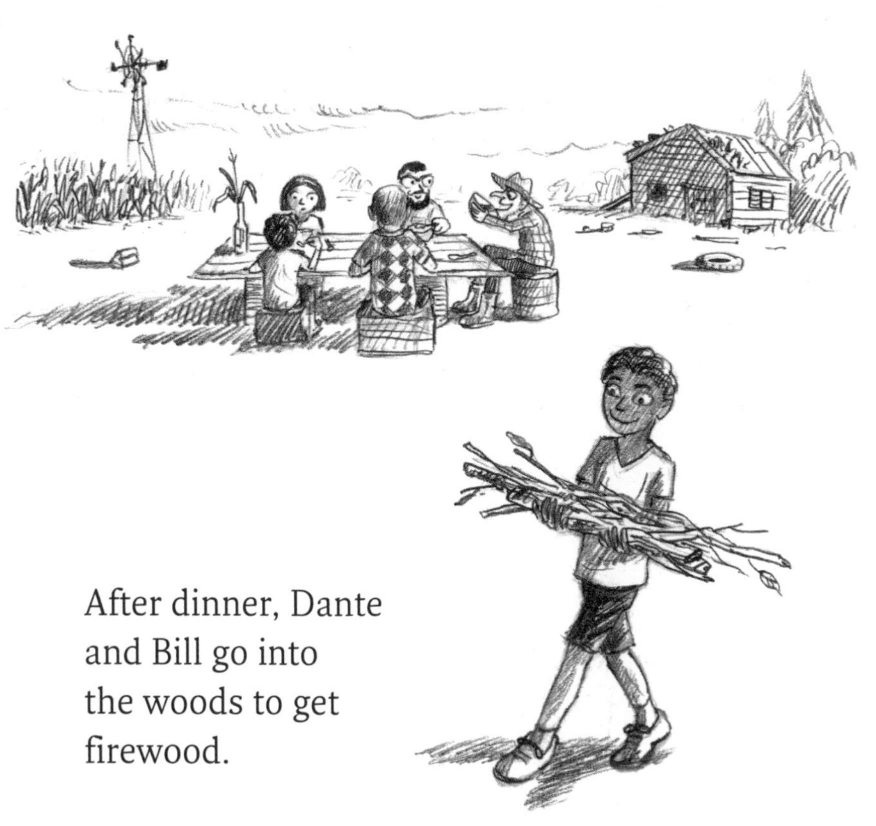

After dinner, Dante and Bill go into the woods to get firewood.

When they come back, Bill makes a little fire.
Then he takes out a can of corn kernels.
"Popcorn?" I ask.
"For DESSERT?"
"Yes, POPCORN!" says Bill.
He puts some kernels in a little pan.
And shows us how it works.

Popping popcorn over an open fire.
I bet they do that in heaven every day.

“We’re going to take a little walk with Bill,” says Steve.
“He wants to talk to us.”
I look at Dante.
Was this his idea?
“Careful with that fire!” Gus calls.
“See you later!”
As soon as they’re gone, I run to our hut.
“FINALLY!” Bob cries.
“Come on out, you whiner,” I say.
“We’re alone.
You don’t have to hide anymore.
And I have a surprise for you.”

CHAPTER 7

ONE? TWO? THREE?

"Ellis?"
I open my eyes.
It's pitch-black in here.
"Yes?"
"Is there any air left in your mattress?"
Dante asks.
I turn over.
Straw and pebbles dig into my hip.
"Oh, no.
Don't say anything to my fathers!
I don't want to go to a hotel."
"Don't worry," says Dante.

"Bill had a talk with them, right?"
I groan.
"I'm not sure that'll help.
They're SO worried about Bill.
They don't want to burden him."
"I'm sure everything will be okay,"
Dante says.
He yawns.
"G'night."
"WHO'S GOING TO A HOTEL?" Bob suddenly roars.
I sit bolt upright.
Dante turns on his flashlight.

We were going to look for my FAMILY, right?

"Yes," mumbles Dante.

"...if they exist, that is."

I frown.

"What do you mean?"

Dante sighs.

"Look, Ellis. You're making such a big deal about your fathers, and what they might do.

And I get scared sometimes.

What if I was wrong about what Coraline said?

That would mean we came to America for nothing.

It would mean we lied to your fathers for nothing!

It would mean Bob has NO family after all!"

And it would be all my fault.

I don't know what to say.
I lie back on my pillow.
Bob stretches out next to my head.
We both stare at the ceiling.
"They exist," Bob finally says.
"I can feel it."

"Dante, we have to get some sleep," I say.
"Things always seem worse at night."
Dante chuckles.
"That's what my mother says whenever
I'm up late, freaking out about
something."
I start laughing too.
"I didn't know you were a worrywart."
"Only at night," he says.

Dante turns off his flashlight.
I fall asleep right away.

My eyes shoot open.
Bob keeps quiet, so I drift off again.

"...two?" Bob suddenly asks.

"...three?"
"Bob," I groan.
"...four?"
"BOB!" Dante and I both shout at once.

"Aaargh," Dante moans. "I'm tired!"
"Corn kernels never get tired," says Bob.

When I wake up again, it's still
pitch-black.
"ZZZZZ," Dante snores.
Bob isn't lying next to me anymore.
"Bob, are you still there?" I ask.
Then I hear him quietly grumbling.
Relieved, I stop holding my breath.
My eyes are getting used to the darkness.
Suddenly I see something big in the room.
It's moving.
We aren't alone!

Bob screams:

"AAAAAAAAH! GET OUT OF HERE!"

I sit straight up.
"What's going on?" Dante shouts.
We both turn on our flashlights.

"The goats are back!" I shout.
"Calm down, Bob.
It's just the goats.
I think we've taken their house."
"Goats are the worst!" Bob screams.
He chases all three of them out.
"Goats hog all the food.
I don't like that."
Dante bursts out laughing.
Bob gives him an angry look.
"They're gone," I say.
"Yes," says Bob with great relief.
He lies down on the floor.
And waves his little arms and legs back and forth.

CHAPTER 8

GOAT PATH

Soon Dante starts snoring again, real loud.
But I can't sleep.
Those poor goats.
We've kicked them out of their house.
As soon as the sky starts to lighten,
I get up.

"Good morning to you too," I say.
I push the curtains aside.
Just in time to see the goats slip under
a fence.

"Guys, the goats have escaped!" I shout.
"Good riddance," says Bob.
I run to the door and yank it open.
The goats are walking into the cornfield, single file.
"Are they allowed to go there?"
"Who cares?" says Bob.

Dante is standing next to me, yawning.
"Looks like they know where they're going," he says.
I shake my head.
"That fence is there for a reason.
Come on, let's go get them."

I quickly pull on my pants.
Outside the air is soft and fresh.
The sun is coming up over the field.
I take a deep breath.
It smells super good here.

Bob scrambles up onto my shoulder.

"So you don't like goats," I say,
"And you're scared to death of chickens."
"Can't you see the hunger in their eyes?"
Bob asks.

Speaking of hunger.
When's breakfast?

The last goat disappears into the field.
"Come on," I say.
"We'll bring the goats back.
Then we'll have breakfast."

Dante and I walk single file, like the goats.
On a narrow path between the cornstalks.

The goat path winds through the field.
The corn plants rise on either side
like walls.
"What a maze," I say.
"Imagine having to wander around here
forever," says Dante.

"I'm hungry," Bob whines.
"Are we there yet?"

The path opens out onto an enormous field.
With blades of grass that come up to our knees.
Bob climbs up onto my shoulder again.
"There are the goats," Dante points.
They're just over there, in the shade of those trees.
But I also see something else...

CHAPTER 9

DON'T EXPLODE AGAIN!

In the distance is a large gray building. Chimneys stick up high in the air.

"Could it be . . . ?" I ask myself out loud.

"THE POPCORN FACTORY!" Dante shouts.

"I saw the same big P on the side of that truck."

"But Bill was going to give us a tour this afternoon," I say.

"We can't just go there now, can we?"

"Of course we can," says Dante.

"All we're going to do is take a little look."

Bob slides off my shoulder.

And climbs up by way of Dante's leg.

"You're the most handsome corn kernel I've ever seen," I tell him.

Bob nods.

"Let's go."

We walk toward the factory.
"Stop!" Bob suddenly yells.
"I don't have anything to give them.
Do you have something?" he asks me.
"A present for my family, like chocolate."
"If Ellis had chocolate," Dante says to Bob,
"you'd have eaten it already."

"Yes, you would," I mutter.
Bob begins to tremble.
"Don't explode now!" I shout.
"You were just so happy!"
But Bob jumps to the ground.
He starts pulling up blades of grass.

Bob doesn't answer.
He pulls on a stinging nettle.
"Ouch!"

"What are you doing?" I shout.

"WHAT DO YOU THINK I'M DOING?" Bob roars.

In the meantime, he grabs hold of a thistle.

OW!

OW!

OW!

POP!

"Let's leave him alone," I tell Dante.
"There's nobody else around anyway."

After a while, Bob calms down.
I tap him on his hat.
"You don't have to give them
anything, Bob.
The fact that you're here is enough.
If other living corn kernels really do exist,
they'll be thrilled to see you."
We walk on through the tall grass.
Suddenly I notice *another* building.

"Is that a chicken coop?" I ask.

Bob scrambles back up my leg
and onto my head.

Chickens?

The coop is surrounded
by a chicken wire fence.

The wire is woven very tight.
So tight that even Bob couldn't get
through.
Suddenly something moves.
"Do you *see* that?" Dante asks.
I nod.
All three of us hold our breath.
Something is moving in there, and it's
NOT a chicken.

CHAPTER 10

A GIRL

We stand there, stock-still.
My eyes are bugging out of my head.
Walking around behind the chicken wire
is a corn kernel.
He's just as big as Bob.
But there's a red bow on his head.

I try to swallow,
but my mouth is dry.
I've known Bob for a long time now.
So I'm used to him.
He's not a human.
He's not an animal.
He's just Bob.
But seeing ANOTHER little creature
exactly like him is weird.
Very weird.
I shake my head.
I can't believe it's real.
"You were right, Bob," I whisper.
"Of course," Bob says.
But Bob isn't moving either.

"Oh, you guys, how cool is this?
It's f-f-f-fantastic!" Dante stammers.
"Shh," I whisper.
"We have to be quiet.
Otherwise we'll frighten him."
"*Her*," says Bob.
"It's definitely a HER."
I smile. I guess for Bob, anybody with a bow in their hair is a girl.
"Okay, let's not frighten *her*."
Dante plops down flat on his belly.
Bob and I do the same.
We crawl through the grass toward the chicken wire.

It makes me think of that field day at school,
when we crawled through the mud.
Farmer Bill chased us.
He kidnapped Bob.
But luckily Bill decided he liked Bob,
and he turned against
Coraline Corn.
From that day
on, he's been
helping us.

Suddenly someone else comes out of the little house.

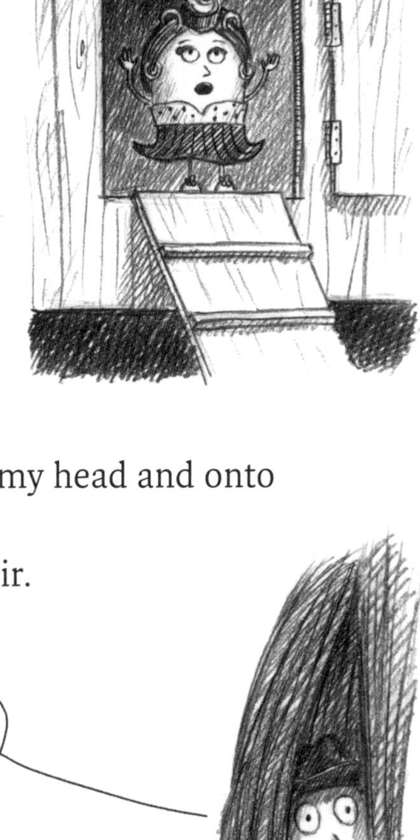

It's a blue corn kernel.
She's wearing a purple dress.
"Another one!" I whisper.
I give Dante a nudge.
Dante looks, and his jaw drops.
The blue corn kernel is waving her arms.
"Ella!" she screams.
Bob quickly slides off my head and onto my shoulder.
He hides under my hair.

"Don't be scared," I say.
"You don't have to hide."
But I dive deeper into the grass myself.
"Ellaaaaaa-la-la-la!" screams the corn lady again.
"Why is she screaming like that?" Dante asks.
"Is she in pain?"
"I think she's singing," says Bob.

"You do?" I ask.
Bob nods his head vigorously.

We stare at the two corn people.
The one with the bow wiggles up and down.

"She's dancing," Bob says in my ear.
"I love dancing too."
"Wow," I mumble.
"Do you think there are...?"
Before I can finish my sentence, even MORE corn kernels come running out!

I count out loud.
"One, two, three, four, five..."

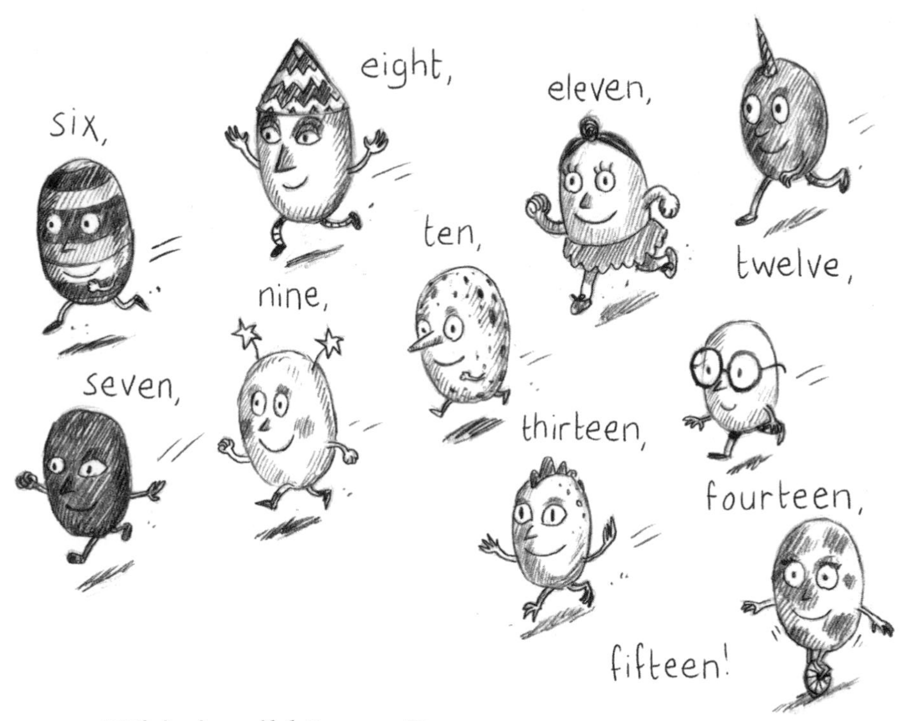
six,
seven,
eight,
nine,
ten,
eleven,
twelve,
thirteen,
fourteen,
fifteen!

"This is wild," says Dante.
"It's completely UNREAL!"
Two other corn kernels start clapping their hands.
The girl with the bow spins around.

I pull Bob off my shoulder.
"Let's take a closer look," I whisper.
But then I see someone coming.
I recognize her right away.

CHAPTER 11

SHE HAS POPCORN!

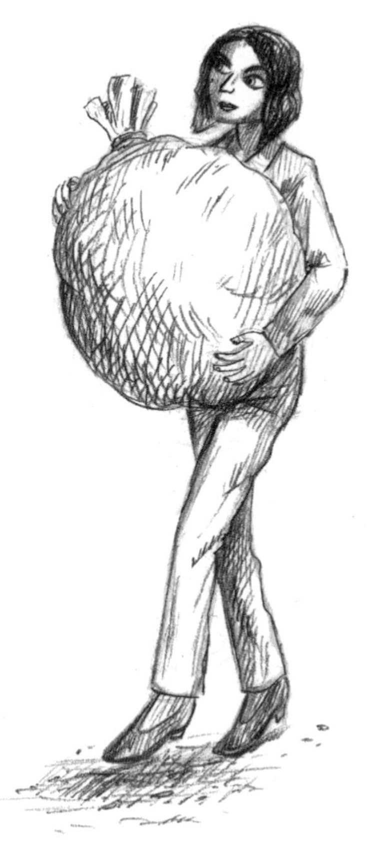

"Coraline," I whisper. Bob hisses like a cat. "What's she doing here?" he spits out. "What's she going to do to my family?" "Take it easy," I say.

BUT I HAVE TO RESCUE THEM!
SHHH!

"The kernels don't look scared, do they?"
Dante whispers.
I shake my head.
"Maybe they just live here, Bob.
Like you live with me.
Let's wait and see what Coraline does."
I don't say anything about the goose
bumps on my arms.

I don't trust Coraline for a second.
She wanted to lock Bob up here too.
When she thought he was dead,
she was happy.
I squeeze my eyes shut.
Why has she come to work so early?
Does she sleep here or something?

A whole load of popcorn
falls into the wire fence.
It rolls around on
the ground like soft
white marbles.

All the corn kernels come running.
I can feel Bob move.
"Wait," I say.
"Stay here."
"But..." Bob whines softly.
"She has popcorn!"
He pulls away and runs
toward the chicken wire.
"No, Bob!" Dante and I
whisper together.

The living corn kernels gobble everything up.
In a few seconds all the popcorn is gone.
Bob turns around and runs back to us.

"They ate it all," he says gloomily.
I pick him up.
"Did you want that awful person to get her hands on you?
She already caught you once.
If she knows you're still alive, she'll never let you go."

Coraline didn't see us.
She looks at the corn kernels and sighs.
Then she turns around and strides back to the factory.
We move forward, slowly and cautiously.
"Caramella!" calls the kernel in the purple dress.
She claps her hands and goes on singing.
The girl with the bow begins to dance.

We creep closer.
There's a door in the wire enclosure.
With a big chain lock on it.
Bob groans.
"They're locked in!
Ellis, they can't get out!
That's not nice!"
"We don't know what's going on yet,"
Dante says.
"But they do exist, Bob!
That's the important thing.
You have a family!
And they're TERRIFIC!
Just look!"

Bob grabs my hand.
"Ellis, this boy doesn't get it.
We have to rescue them.
NOW!"
"It's not that easy," I say.
"Where would we hide them?
We need a plan.
My fathers are probably worried.
They don't know where we are.
We HAVE to go back to the farm first."
Bob nods, but I can tell it's hard for him.
"Then we can also have breakfast,"
I continue.
He brightens up right away.
"After that we'll come back," I promise.
"And then we can get to know your
family."
Bob turns around.
"Okay, breakfast first."

But only because it's the most important meal of the day.
You should NEVER skip breakfast.

CHAPTER 12

NO HAIR

My fathers are standing in the farmyard,
next to their suitcases.
They look worried.
Oh, no. This is not good.
This is REALLY not good!
I slap on my honest face.
"Yoo-hoo, here we are!" I call out to them.
"We went for a little walk.
One minute. I have to put something away."

We run into
our hut.

"Uh...Ellis," says Bob as soon as we get inside.

Didn't you forget something? What about breakfast?!

"Just stay put, Bob," I say.
"I'll bring you a couple of sandwiches."
Bob shakes his head.
"I'm HUNGRY.
And I'm way too excited.
We just discovered my family!
I'll crawl into your pocket.
Then you can sneak me a few bites."
"Bob!" I shout.
"Stop going on about food!
My fathers have packed their bags.
They probably want to go to a hotel.
Don't you see?

I have no idea how I would hide you there.
I can't start telling even MORE lies."
"I'm NOT going to a hotel!" Bob yells.
"Not by the hair of my chinny-chin-chin!"
Then Dante pipes up.
"You have *no* hair on your chin, Bob.
Or anywhere else on your head."

"Oh, no," he says.
They both burst out laughing.
I stare at them and sigh.
"All right, come on."
Bob crawls into my pocket.

The table in the farmyard is set for breakfast.
My fathers look serious.
"We were very worried, Ellis," says Gus.
"All of a sudden, you guys just disappeared.
There are probably lots of wild animals around here."
"Exactly," says Steve.
"Bears and snakes and things!
We're not in Holland anymore.
If you want to go anywhere, you have to ask permission."
"But it was super early!" I shout.

Just then I see the goats.
Strolling out of the cornfield as easy as you please.
And squirming back under the fence.
I point to them.
"Do you think they're dangerous too?
Because all we saw were goats.
Right, Dante?"
"And corn," he says with a grin.
"LOTS AND LOTS of corn."

"Hey, it's Bill!" Dante suddenly shouts.
He runs up to him.
They stand there whispering together.
Then Bill's eyes start to sparkle.
First he looks at the cornfield,
and then at me.

I smile back and nod.
Wow for sure.
They really *do* exist,
that's what *that* means.
Bob isn't the only living corn kernel!

Suddenly I feel a whole lot lighter.
We found them!
That's what this was all about.
That's why we came here.
Bob is right: we have to rescue them.
That Coraline is dangerous.
"Can we eat soon?" I ask.
"I'm starving!"

CHAPTER 13

A LITTLE SHOP

I pour syrup on my pancakes. Meanwhile my fathers are having a talk with Bill. They don't see me shoving bits of food into my pocket.

Suddenly my eye falls on their suitcases. Right.

What are your suitcases doing there?
I don't want to go to a hotel!

Steve looks at me with surprise.
"To a hotel?" he asks.
"Whatever gave you that idea?"
Gus nods at Bill.
"We're going to do some work for Bill, remember?"
"Oh," I say.
"But I thought that..."
Steve explains.
"Last night we made plans with Bill.
He wants to open a shop."

Right, Bill? A little shop?

"That's right!" says Bill, laughing.
He gives Dante a wink.
A shop? Was that Dante's idea?
Dante looks at me with a grin.
So *that's* why he wasn't worried.

"Bill is going to sell his own popcorn,"
says Gus.
"Made from his own corn.
In EVERY flavor!"
He stares dreamily into space.
"Salty, sweet, caramel, cheese, pepper,
curry, pizza..."

"Uh, darling..." says Steve.
"I think she gets it.
LOTS AND LOTS of popcorn flavors."
"Yes," says Gus.
"Isn't this great?"

My fathers go on and on about their work.
They pay no attention to me.
Meanwhile I keep stashing food in my pocket.
All that talk about popcorn…
It's making Bob very hungry.
"We're going to help build the shop," says Gus.
Steve nods.
"And we'll make a great big rubber ducky on a tall pole.
So you can see it from miles away."
"To attract customers?" Dante asks.
Steve nods.
"Take a look at this."

"But what about those suitcases?" I ask again.

Gus shrugs.

"Our room is too small for the suitcases. So we're putting them somewhere else."

"Not in the hut with us," I say.

Gus laughs.

"Yeah, okay, we get it, Ellis."

We're putting the suitcases in the shed.

I am SO relieved!
I cram an extra big piece of pancake into my pocket for Bob.
But he doesn't touch it.
His little arms suddenly feel as floppy as wet noodles.
Oh, no.
I jump up and pull Dante along with me.
"We have to go to the kitchen NOW," I whisper.
"Is something wrong?" he whispers back.
I nod.
"Hey, are you guys full already?" Gus calls out.
"Yes, well, uh, we have to..."
Dante runs to the table.
He grabs our plates.

CHAPTER 14

QUICK! INTO THE MICROWAVE!

When we get to the kitchen, I pull Bob out of my pocket.

He's lying in my hand, pale and limp.

"Quick," I say.

"Where's the microwave?"

We look around the kitchen.

What a mess!

"There!"

Dante opens the little door.

The plate inside is really dirty.

But it will have to do.

I carefully lay Bob down on all the crumbs.
Sometimes he has to go into the microwave to get himself charged.
But right now he looks very bad.
"I've never seen him so pale," I say.
"It must have been all the excitement," says Dante.
"Suddenly he has a whole new family. That's a lot to process."
I close the door.
"How do you start this thing?"
I push one of the buttons.
But nothing happens.
The stupid thing doesn't work!

Then I see another button.
"Of course," I say.
I push "start." 
But *still* nothing happens.
Now Dante is almost as pale as Bob.
"I'll go get Bill," he says.
I'm almost choking.
All I can do is nod, and Dante tears out of the kitchen.
Then I see the cord.
Suddenly my voice is back.
"The plug!" I shout.

Dante comes back in.
"What?"
I push the plug into the socket and press "start."
Right away the microwave starts zooming.
I bite my thumbnail.
Dante counts to sixty.
"Now!" he says.
I jerk the door open.
Will Bob be back to his old self?

Dante slaps me on the shoulder.
"Good job!"
"Are you okay?" Bob asks.

I giggle.
"I don't think so.
People don't belong in microwaves.
Only corn kernels."
"Man, you really scared us!" Dante says to Bob.
"You feeling better now?"
Bob gives us a thumbs-up.

"Perfecto!"

"Hey, look at this!"

My eye has fallen on a pair of wire cutters.

"These look pretty sturdy."

Dante nods slowly.

"You could easily cut through wire with them."

I wiggle my eyebrows up and down.

"Are you thinking what I'm thinking?"

"What are you thinking?" Bob asks. "What wire?"

I wiggle my eyebrows some more.

Bob stares at me.

It finally clicks.
"Aaah, the chicken wire!" Bob shouts.
"Around the coop!
We're going to rescue my family!"
He wiggles his nose.
Dante looks at us and shakes his head.
"You guys are weird.
Come on.
We're going back to the factory."

CHAPTER 15

CHICKEN WIRE, HERE WE COME!

First we walk through the cornfield.
Then we crawl through the grass, very cautiously.
There's no one near the coop.
No goats, no Coraline.
But no corn kernels either.
"Aren't they home?" Bob asks.
"They're probably inside," I say.
Dante snaps the wire cutters open and shut.

Chicken wire, here we come.

Bob climbs up my leg.
"Yeah, chicken wire, here we come!"
Suddenly he stops climbing.
He's clinging to my waist.
I pick him up gently.
"Exciting, huh?"
"No big deal," he squeaks.
I hold him close to my chest.
"You hear that?
My heart is pounding too."

Dante tries to cut the chicken wire.
But it's very strong.
The cutters keep sliding off.
"Squeeze harder," says Bob.
"Oh, *right*," says Dante.
"Thanks for the tip."

"Bob, I'm doing my best, okay?"
"You just have to squeeze HARDER," says Bob.
Dante huffs.

I grab the wire cutters too and we both squeeze together.
It works! Now there's a hole in the chicken wire.
We look at each other and smile.
Dante wiggles *his* eyebrows.
"Well, well, well," I shout.
He grins.
We climb through the hole.
"Did you hear that?" I whisper as we get closer to the coop.
It sounds like cooing and chirping.
As if a whole flock of birds were inside.
I peer through the doorway.

Now I'm getting a good look at them.
I saw them this morning too.
But that was from far away.
Now I see that they're all different.
Some are blue.
Others are orange or striped.
I also see a couple that are plain yellow.
Just like Bob.
But all of them are so...alive!
So real!

Bob slides off my shoulder.
He runs inside.
When he gets to the middle of the coop
he stops.

HELLO, FAMILY!

The corn kernels are
scared to death.

"EEEEEEK!"
"Aaaah!"
Pop! Pop!

Two of the kernels even change into giant
pieces of popcorn.
They bounce all over the place.

CHAPTER 16

WEIRD GUYS THESE CORN KERNELS

Dante and I rush inside.

"Calm down," I say to the kernels gently.

"Take it easy, *shhhh*."

"Hello, everyone!" says Dante.

"We're friends!"

He glances at Bob.

"...family," he says.

Cautiously, the kernels come closer to us.

They start chirping again, very softly.

And cooing.

I recognize the kernel with the bow.
I slowly lower myself and squat down beside her.
"Hello," I say with a smile.
"I'm Ellis. And who are you?"
The girl laughs back.
She begins rattling something off in a foreign language.
It's full of those strange bird sounds.
I look at Dante.
"Do you understand what she's saying?"

It sounds a little like English. But not quite.

Bob gives me an angry look.
"Why don't they just speak Dutch, like we do?"
"I can't do anything about that," I say.
"We're in America!"
But to be fair,
I hadn't thought about it either.
If they don't speak English...
then Dante can't translate what they're saying.
How are we going to understand each other?
But Bob has forgotten the language problem.
He's looking at the girl with the bow.
And she's looking back.
As if they were the only ones in the coop.

Bob holds the flower out to her.
“Bob,” he says.
“Popcorn Bob.”
“Caramella,” says the girl.
“Popcorn Caramella.”
She takes the flower.
“Cara...mella,” says Bob.
As if he were tasting her name.
Looks like it tastes pretty good.
I’ve NEVER seen Bob grin like this before.

We sit down in the middle of the coop.
The corn kernels gather round.
“We...are...friends,” I say, smiling.

"We come from far away," I say.
I shape my hands into a heart for "friends."
I pause, and Dante tries to translate, also smiling.
"From *fa-a-a-r* away."
I gesture more, hoping they understand.
"Ellis . . . Dante . . . from Holland.
A *sm-a-a-all* country. Very *fa-a-a-r* away.
On the *o-o-other* side of the ocean."
One black corn kernel bursts out laughing.

Soon all the other kernels are rolling with laughter.
"I guess they think we're funny," says Dante.
"Oh," I say.
"Okay."

One of the kernels stands up.
He clears his throat.
And waves his arms in the air.

UNDEE U-U-U-UHDDER SITE UFF DEE OSHOON!

It sounds like Dante's English translation of my words.
But different.
The other kernels crack up again.

"I think he's mimicking me," Dante whispers.
I cross my arms.
"Wow, that is so rude.
Weird guys, these corn kernels."

Now a purple kernel presses something into my hand.
Dante and Bob each get something too.
They're pieces of vegetables.
I get raw cauliflower.
Dante and Bob get carrots.
I put on my sweetest smile.
"Thank you!"
I look at the cauliflower.
"Very healthy," I mutter.
"Ms. Kim would be proud." (That's our health-obsessed teacher.)
"Delicious," says Bob.
He wipes his mouth.
The kernels look at me with expectation.
I take a quick bite.

The kernels cheer.

CHAPTER 17

ELLIS-THE-BELLIS

The blue corn kernel with the dress is singing.

She's waving her little arms.

"That is..." Dante mumbles.

"Loud," says Bob.

I bite my lip to keep from laughing.

The other kernels form a circle around the singer.
They yodel a kind of song.
The applause sounds like popcorn.
"Well, I think it's really great," says Bob.
"But, uh..."

When are we going to rescue them?

"Soon," I say.
Dante looks doubtful.
"They don't exactly look unhappy, do they?
I think they really like it here."
"But Coraline has them locked up!" I say out loud.
Suddenly everyone is silent.

All the corn kernels look at me.
Dante shrugs his shoulders.
“Maybe the chicken wire is there to protect them.”
I roll my eyes.
“From what? The goats?”
Dante sighs.
“I don’t know either!
If only we could communicate with them.”
Suddenly he grabs his backpack.

I have an idea.
I'm going to teach them.

Dante takes his sketchbook out of his bag.
And then a pencil.
"Oh, yeah," he says.
"And I brought these, too."
He pulls out a big bag of chocolate candies and passes them around.
The corn kernels make happy little noises.

"Dante, you're my hero," Bob says with his mouth full.

"Yeah, right," I mutter.
"First BILL is your hero.
Then DANTE.
What about me?"

"Oh, come on, Ellis," says Bob.
"You know I love you."

I giggle.

"Let's go, Dante," Bob says between bites.

Hurry up and teach them Dutch.

Dante shakes his head no.
"I'm going to teach them *English*, Bob."
"But why?" I ask.
"Because I think it would be easier for them.
It sounds like they already know a few English words."
"And what about us?" I shout.
"Bob and I can't speak English!"
"I can," says Bob.
"Just listen:

"That means JA," he says to Caramella, in Dutch.
She smiles.

"Just practice with the kernels," Dante says to me.
He claps his hands.
"Come on, we're going outside.
The English lesson is about to begin!"
The corn kernels look at Dante with curious faces.
He draws something.
Then he clearly pronounces each word.

"HOUSE," we all say.

"FACTORY," we all say together.

"DANGER."

"BOSS."

"ESCAPE."

"FARM."

"CORN."

Boy, this is hard!
Dante draws one word
after another.
The corn kernels are panting.
After a while, my blood
begins to boil.
"Come on, Ellis-the-Bellis!"
says Dante.
"Read all the words out loud again,
one after the other, real fast."
That's the last straw.
My head is sizzling.
I stamp my feet.
"I HATE reading out rows of words."

AND I HATE IT WHEN YOU CALL ME ELLIS-THE-BELLIS!!!

The corn kernels
explode too.

Suddenly I feel a tiny bit stupid.
I'm not a corn kernel, am I?
But just when I'm about to apologize,
I hear something.
No, not *something*.
Someone. Talking.
And she's coming our way.
"Coraline," I whisper.

CHAPTER 18

SORRY I EXPLODED

Dante and I hide behind the coop.

"Bob?" I whisper.

"Get over here!"

"He's still with the other kernels," Dante says quietly.

“But I don’t think you can tell them apart. Not when they’ve all popped.”
Dante peers around the corner.
“Can you see him?” I ask quietly.
“Yes, he’s over there.”
I gently pull Dante aside.

“Why does Coraline look so angry?” I whisper.
“And I’m sorry I exploded too, by the way.”
Just then Coraline starts yelling something.

"What's she screaming about?" I whisper.
"*Stop exploding!*" Dante translates.
I shake my head.
"Oh, come on.
They're corn kernels. Of course they explode."
"Shh," says Dante.
"Let me listen. She's saying something else."

"You... disgusting little insects!
Ugly little greedy guts!
Bloated little maggots!"

Dante has to struggle to understand Coraline.
She's talking SO fast!
"She used the same growth potion that Bill tried once," he whispers.
"Remember? He told us about it.
She wanted to sell popcorn that was as big as apples.
But then they came to life.
That's why she's so angry.
No one wants to eat live popcorn, she says."
Coraline thunders on.
Dante turns to me with a look of horror.
"What?" I whisper. "What's she saying?"
"She says that tomorrow she'll be rid of them.
FOREVER."

Coraline storms back to the factory.
Soon she's out of sight.
The blood is pounding in my ears.
"She is really awful," I say.
"We've got to get out of here."
I run to Bob.
"Did you hear what that horrible person said?" I ask.
"Of course," says Bob with his know-it-all voice.
"My English is super good, Ellis.
She said she's going to make new popcorn."
I shake my head.
"It's not nice to lie, Bob.
It's better to be honest."

Suddenly I feel hot all over.
My cheeks are turning red.
"Lying to my fathers is different!" I shout.

Dante chuckles.
"And to make popcorn whenever you want."
I clench my fists.
"Oh, forget it," says Dante.
We quickly tell Bob what Coraline said.
He starts swelling.
"No!" I tell him. "Don't get angry again!
Listen, all the kernels have to get out of here.
Right away."

I rush to the hole in the chicken wire.
"Come on!" I shout.
"You can leave through this hole!"
But the kernels just stand there.
"Hello!" I shout.
"You're all in danger!
Coraline wants to get rid of you!
Come with us!"
Dante translates.
But no one moves.
Not even Bob.

CHAPTER 19

IT'S DANGEROUS HERE

Someone says something in English.
I look at Dante and then at Bob.
But they both look at Caramella.
She skips up to me.

I bend down
and stick out
my hand.
She jumps
onto my palm.

“She’s speaking English!” I shout.

“What is she saying?” I ask.
“She’s saying *danger*,” says Dante, in Dutch, of course.
“YES, *danger*!” cries Bob.
He runs up my pants leg and down my arm.
And gives Caramella a hug.
“*Danger*!
Ellis, did you hear that?
Danger.
Pretty good, huh?”

Caramella talks to Dante.
He looks proud.
"She sure is a fast learner!
She knows ALL the words I drew.
And she understands what I'm saying!"
"Very smart," I say.
"SMART?" Bob cries.
"She's a GENIUS!"
He looks at Caramella and says:

"She wants to know where they're supposed to go," says Dante.

"Anywhere in the world but here?" I suggest.

Dante looks uneasy.

"But this is their home!

She says Coraline doesn't treat them badly.

They get food every day.

And all they have to do is dance and sing."

Caramella spins around in my hand.

Bob looks at her with astonishment.

"And she does it SO beautifully!"

I give Dante a questioning look.

"They *have* to dance and sing? Why would Coraline want them to do that?"

Dante listens to Caramella.
"She doesn't know," he says.
"She says sometimes she has to go into a little cabinet."
"A cabinet?" I ask.
I'm getting angry again.
Dante shakes his head.
"Actually she likes it.
I think she means the microwave.
Because after that she feels fit again, she says."
I nod.
"Aha. So she has to get charged every now and then, just like Bob."

After that I always feel tip-top!

"But almost every kitchen has a microwave," I say.

"That's no reason to stay here.

Tell her that.

Coraline said that after tomorrow she'll be rid of them.

FOREVER!

So they have to get out of here by TONIGHT!"

Dante translates my words into English.

Caramella nods.

“We have to talk to Bill NOW,” I say. “Maybe the corn kernels can live with him.”
Dante quickly gathers up his stuff. “Good plan.”
I put Caramella on the ground.

Bob starts to follow her, but I grab him.
“Let me go, Ellis!” Bob growls in my hands.
“Dante,” I shout. “Tell Caramella to explain this to the others.
And tell her we’ll be right back.”
I dive through the hole in the chicken wire.

"What about your fathers?" Dante asks.
He runs after me and Bob.
"No idea," I yell.
I've been lying to them about Bob ever since I first met him.
Is it time to tell them the truth?
But what if they get angry?
Or even worse: what if they don't let Bob stay with me anymore?

CHAPTER 20

WE'LL BE RIGHT BACK!

Gasping for breath, we run into the farmyard.
It's even more of a mess than before.
My fathers are sitting right in the middle of it.
They look up.
"Hey, there you are.
Got a goat on your tail?" Steve jokes.

"Look, you guys!" says Gus.
"The duck is finished."
It's really coming along.
"And what have you been up to?"
Dante and I look
at each other.
We shrug our
shoulders.

"Where's Bill?"
I ask.
"Around here
somewhere,"
says Steve.
He points with his chin.
"Hey," Gus says.
"If you guys decide to make more campfire
popcorn, count me in!"
I nod.
It seems like ages since we did that.

We find Bill behind the farmhouse.
Dante doesn't have to talk him into it.
He says yes right away.

"Did you hear that, Bob?
It's all settled."
"Bill, buddy," says Bob.
They give each other
a fist bump.
But then Bill says he wants to give us a lift in his truck.
"To the factory?" I ask.
"I don't think that'll work.
We'll stand out too much."
Dante hesitates.
"How else are we going to bring fifteen living corn kernels back here?"
I bite my lip.
"I dunno. Walk?"
"What if we park further away?" Dante suggests.

We walk past my fathers.

Where are you guys going?

Bill waves with
his car keys.
"He's going to
show us the popcorn factory," I say.
"Fun, huh?"
I hold my breath.
Are they going to believe me?
I look as honest as I can.
Steve puts down his brush.
"It's the weekend," says Gus.
"The factory will be closed, won't it?"
"We'll just look from a distance,"
Dante says.
I smile.

"We'll be right back. Bye!"
This time all of us can sit up front in Bill's truck.
He drives like a maniac!
We tear over the narrow roads.
Sand and gravel fly in every direction.
We reach the factory in no time.

The factory grounds look abandoned.
But maybe Coraline is still inside.
Bill parks the car behind a bush.
We sneak around the factory in a big circle.

As soon as he sees the corn kernels, Bill starts jumping up and down.
"I think he likes them," I say.
Bill motions to the kernels to come with us.
"Come on, guys," says Dante.
"This is Bill.
You can live with him.
Our truck is parked a little further on."
The corn kernels chirp louder than ever.
"Come on!" I shout.

The corn kernels start waving their arms wildly.
But they do come with us.
"Caramella took care of everything," I say.
One by one, the kernels hop onto the grass.

Bob taps my leg.
"Where's Caramella?"
I look down.
"Yes. Where *is* she?"

Now I see that the corn kernels aren't just waving.
They're pointing.

Oh, no.
They're pointing to the factory.
I point too.
"Is she in there?"

"Did someone take her away?"
Dante asks.
"Maybe she just needed the microwave."
Bob gives me a threatening look.
"We're not going anywhere without Caramella."
"Of course not," I say.
We have no choice.
We have to get into the factory.
And sneak Caramella out.

"You guys wait here," I gesture to the other corn kernels.
"We'll be right back.
WITH Caramella."

CHAPTER 21

IN THE FACTORY

Bill shows us a door at the back of
the factory.
Dante and I press our ears against it.
It's warm from the sun.
All I can hear are the crickets in the grass.
Nothing else.

Bob starts tugging at the hairs on my neck.

"Ouch," I mumble.

"What are you doing?" he asks impatiently.

"You open a door with your *hands*."

Bill fiddles with the handle.

"It's probably locked," I whisper.

But the door easily swings open.

I wipe my sweaty palms on my pants.

Bill waves us inside.

We leave the door open just a crack.
That gives us a little light.
And we can get out fast if we have to.
We're standing in a long, narrow corridor.
It's dark and cool inside.
We walk a bit further without making a sound.
Past shelves and boxes.
And every now and then we pass a door.
They're all locked.
The corridor opens out into a big room.
Cautiously we peek inside.

Sunlight is pouring in from high windows
onto a group of silver tanks.
The tanks are as big as cars.
Bill says something to Dante.
"That's where the kernels are popped,"
he whispers.
"Thousands at a time."
We walk past a big conveyor belt.
It's not running.
I keep looking around me.
"Where could Caramella be?" I whisper.
"Caramella!" Bob shouts.
"*Shhh*," we all answer back.
We tiptoe through the big room as fast
as we can.
At the end is another door.
We peer through a little window.
Behind it is another world.

At first all I can see is
white light.
It's coming from
bright bulbs mounted
on the ceiling.
There are white
containers spread
across several counters.
Fluid is gurgling in glass beakers
and tubes.
"It's a laboratory," I whisper.
"A what?" asks Bob.
"Where they do tests and experiments,"
Dante explains.
"Weird," I say.
"A laboratory in a popcorn factory."
Bill looks surprised too.
Suddenly we see Coraline.
"Duck!" I whisper.
"Fast!"
We crawl away on our hands and knees.
I pull Dante behind a machine.
Bill dives behind another contraption.

But he loses his hat.
My heart almost stops!
The door opens, and Coraline Corn walks into the room.
Has she seen us?

Coraline is staring at her phone.
We slip into the laboratory behind her back.
But right away we have to hide again.
There's someone else in here!
A short woman, also wearing a white suit.
She's standing with her back to us.

"Ellis," Bob whispers in my ear.
"Look up there."

Up on a shelf is a row of cages.
They're no bigger than tea mugs.
And they're all empty, except for one.
Inside it is Caramella.
It's such a tiny cage.
If she popped, it would never hold her.
My blood begins to boil.
How DARE they lock her up like this!
Bob is trembling too.
Before I can do anything, he slips away.
He runs across the floor and climbs up to the shelf.
As fast as a mouse.

Clink-clank.
Bob rattles the door of the cage.
The assistant sees him right away.
She grabs a kind of butterfly net and races up to him.
Bill jumps to his feet.
"BOB!" Dante and I roar.
And then everything happens all at once.

CHAPTER 22

RUN, RUN, RUN!

The assistant lets out a piercing scream.
She knocks over a glass beaker.
It smashes to the floor.
Shards of glass fly in all directions.
This gives us just enough time to
take action.
We reach the shelf sooner than she does.
I grab Bob.
And Dante seizes the little cage with
Caramella inside.
"Run, run, run!" I shout.

We race through the big room.
I zigzag past the tanks
and take a quick look behind me.
Oh, no.
Now Coraline Corn is after us too.

Suddenly Dante and I find ourselves cornered by Coraline and her assistant.
There's no way out.
I can't see Bill anywhere.
Coraline is standing right in front of us.
I can tell that she knows who we are.
I hold onto Bob even tighter.

Coraline starts talking.
"She says we're thieves," Dante quickly translates.
"That all the corn kernels are *hers*."
I take a step forward.
Should I just slip past her?
But Coraline stretches out her arms.
She takes a phone out of her pocket and hands it to her assistant.
Dante quietly translates what she's saying.
"*I'm keeping an eye on those kids.*
You call that man.
Tell him to come.

Not tomorrow. Now.
Things are getting out of control here."
"What man?" I ask.
Dante looks shocked.

"She's sold the kernels to a man.
She said something about Las Vegas.
Where they put on lots of shows.
The kernels will have to dance and sing there."
Caramella says something to Dante.
"But they want to keep Caramella," Dante translates.
"To take part in experiments!"
I'm holding Bob so tightly I almost squeeze him in half.
Suddenly I see Bill on the other side of the room.
He looks helpless.
"BILL!" I yell.
"Get Gus and Steve!
Dante, tell him to go get my fathers!"

I'm steaming with rage.
My head is pounding.
Shows?
Experiments?
There's ringing in my ears.
I'm SO angry!

And then . . . I blow up.

My first explosion was nothing compared to this.

NOW I'm REALLY mad.

But I'm not the only one.

Dante is furious too.

And Bob and Caramella both explode.

Caramella even bursts out of her little cage.

Suddenly I see the other living corn kernels.

"You guys wait outside!" I shout.

But it's too late. They're also starting to explode.

At first Coraline and her assistant look puzzled.

But then they begin clutching at the angry popcorns flying all around them.

They manage to catch a few.

But before they know it, all the popcorns have joined in the attack.

I run up to a
control panel
full of buttons
and sliders.
I bet this is
what they use
to run all the
machines.

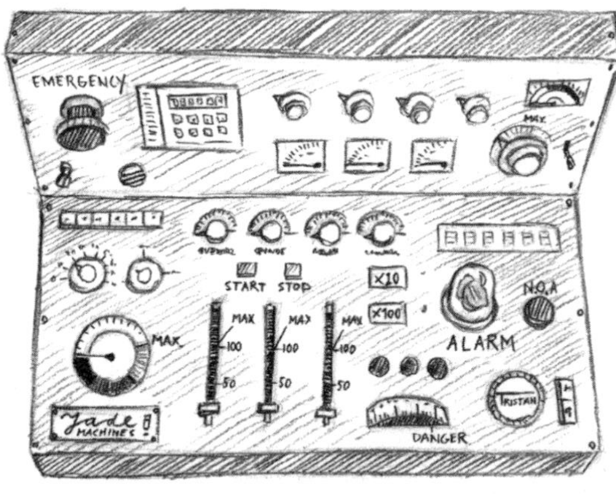

But how does it work?
I remember Bill's microwave.
Should I just press START?
Immediately a green light goes on.
Dante and I push all the sliders to the top.
Thousands of corn kernels pour into
the tanks.

Then another load.
And another…
There must be
MILLIONS of
kernels in there!

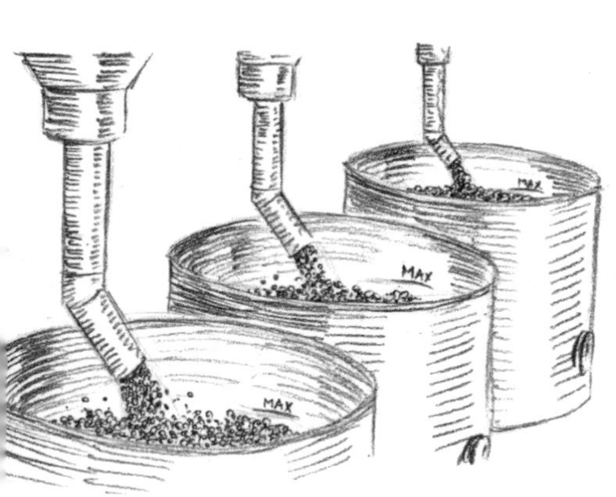

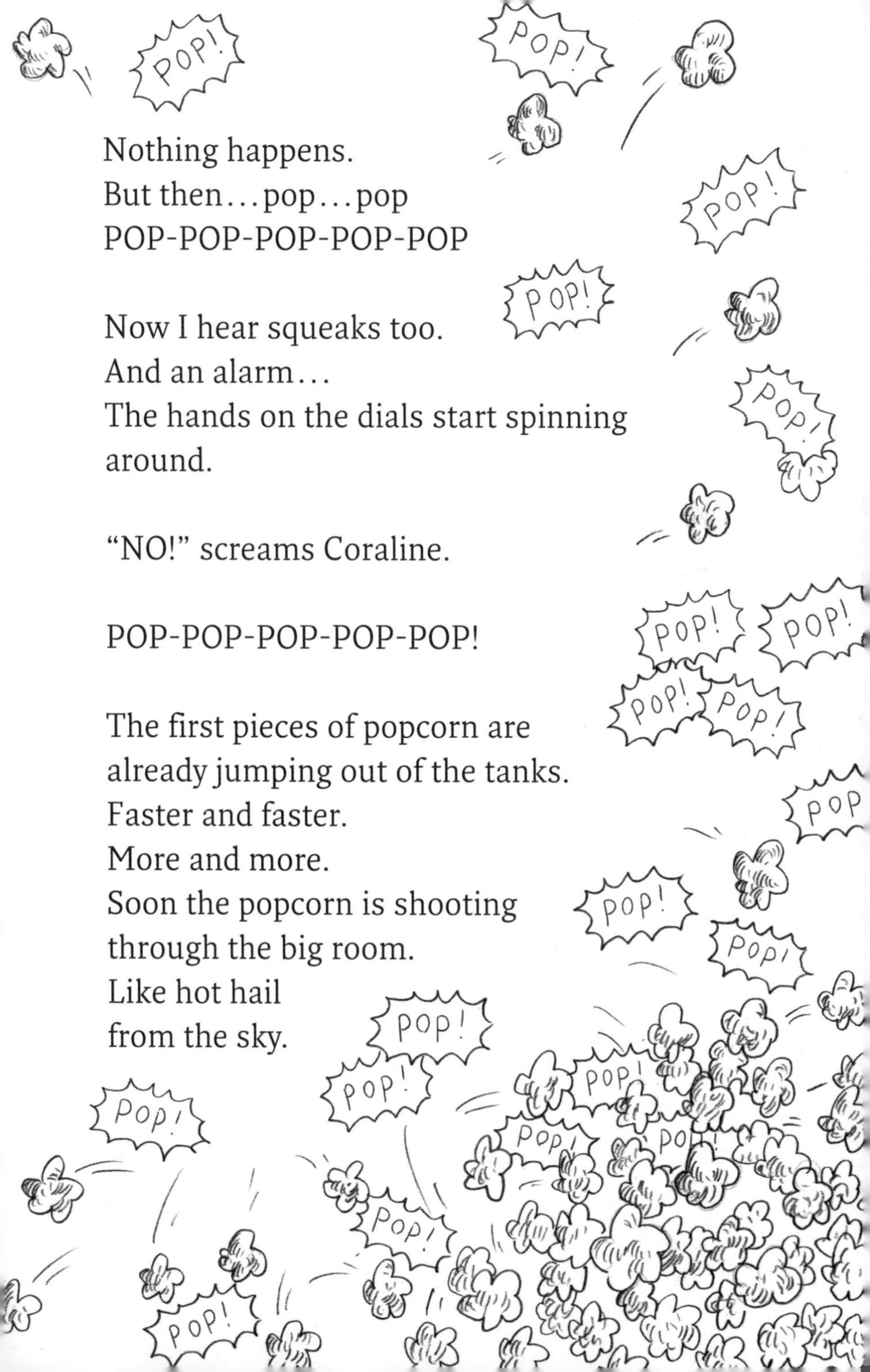

Nothing happens.
But then…pop…pop
POP-POP-POP-POP-POP

Now I hear squeaks too.
And an alarm…
The hands on the dials start spinning around.

“NO!” screams Coraline.

POP-POP-POP-POP-POP!

The first pieces of popcorn are already jumping out of the tanks.
Faster and faster.
More and more.
Soon the popcorn is shooting through the big room.
Like hot hail
from the sky.

"Let them go! Now!" I shout.

Coraline and her assistant race out of the room.

"RUN!" roars Dante.

We all tear into the other corridor.

And then I see the rear exit.

Dante and I chase all the living popcorns outside.

We run after them, into the field.

Soon there's popcorn EVERYWHERE.

POP
POP
POP
POP
POP
POP
POP
POP
POP
POP
POP
POP
POP
POP
POP
POP
POP
POP
POP
POP
POP
POP
POP
POP
POP
POP
POP
POP
POP
POP

CHAPTER 23

POPCORN FIREWORKS

As we run through the field, a million pounds of popcorn explode into the air behind us.
The smell is SO strong.
A movie theater is nothing compared to this.
I take a quick look around.
A big white wave is rolling toward us.

“Watch out!” I scream.
“Or we’ll be buried in popcorn!”
“Run!” Dante shouts to the corn kernels.
“As fast as you can!”
But they can’t run fast on their
tiny little legs.
Then I see Bill’s goats.

“Climb up on their backs!” I shout to the corn kernels.
“Are you nuts?” shouts Bob.
“I hate goats!”

Bob and Caramella climb up on the biggest goat.
In a flash, the rest of the kernels find their own goats to sit on.
"Follow me!" I shout.
"To the farm!"
But the goats don't listen.

They race helter-skelter through the corn plants.
Soon we're lost.

“Where’s the path?” I call to Dante.
“We’ll never get out of here this way!”
“Look up!” Bob shouts.
“Up there, Ellis!”
My eyes are watering from the smoke.
And the smell of popcorn.
It’s hard to make
anything out.
And then I see it.

The popcorn rubber ducky is enormous.
He's at the top of a tall pole.
And he's showing us the way.
I steer the goats in the right direction.
Soon the air becomes fresher.
And in a little while, we come thundering out of the cornfield.

My fathers run up to us.
Farmer Bill cheers.
Without saying a word, I fall into my fathers' arms.
"Oh, honey, are you okay?" Gus asks.
Steve pulls
Dante into our
little circle.
"And how
about you?"
"I'm fine,"
Dante
mumbles.
"We were just
about to jump
in the car,"
says Steve.
He's as white
as a sheet.

"Bill was totally panicking.
He said you two were in danger."
"What happened?" my fathers ask together.

For a minute I'm tempted to put on my honest face.
It's automatic.
My happy eyes.
My sweet smile.
But I decide not to.
It's not an honest face at all.
It's the face of a liar.
I pull away from their hug.
And point to the living corn kernels.
"Dads, this is my friend Bob.
And that is his family."

CHAPTER 24

WE TELL THE WHOLE STORY

We talk and talk.
And we eat.
And we eat some more.
Almost all evening.
By then, my fathers know EVERYTHING.
Gus points to Bob.
"Did you really think
we would take him
away from you?"

I shrug my shoulders.
"You took the regular popcorn away from me."
"When did we do that?" asks Steve.
"When we were supposed to eat more healthy food, remember?" I say.
"And then that Coraline came after Bob.
And then Bob wanted to search for his family.
And then . . . and then . . ."
I take a deep breath.
"Then I just couldn't stop lying.
I got really good at it."
I grin.
"At first I thought I was only super good at making popcorn."
Bob runs up to us.
"But that's not true!"

She's also super good at doing handstands.

My father snuggles with me again.
"I'm sorry," he murmurs.

Popcorn is fantastic. Just as great as rubber duckies. I want to get to know them all.

That evening we put the goats back in their stable. And we all camp in the farmyard. We make popcorn.
We lie on our blankets, under the stars.
And we tell the whole story all over again.

The next day flies by.
And so do the weeks that follow.
The popcorn factory is closed down.
We haven't heard a word from Coraline.

Ellis, we need a new batch of popcorn!

At Bill's shop, business is booming.
We make the best popcorn
in America.
And that's no accident!
We all work very hard.

And when I say that we all work hard,
I mean ALL OF US.

But we keep the corn kernel family
a secret.
Because just imagine
if somebody from Las Vegas were to come
to the door!

After four weeks, we have to go back to Holland.

THE END*

*Well, not quite…

Welcome home, Caramella.

HUNGRY FOR MORE

TURN THE PAGE
TO FILL UP!

READ THE BOOKS
THAT STARTED IT ALL!

BOOK 2

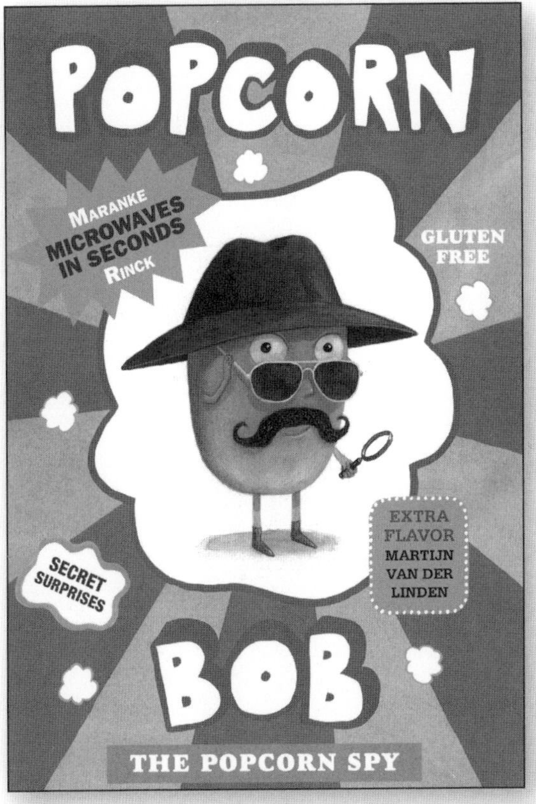
POPCORN
MARANKE
MICROWAVES IN SECONDS
RINCK
GLUTEN FREE
EXTRA FLAVOR
MARTIJN VAN DER LINDEN
SECRET SURPRISES
BOB
THE POPCORN SPY